In the Kitchen with Solids, Liquids, and Gases

Chrissa Bloom

REAL LIFE readers™

Rosen Classroom™
New York

Solids, **liquids**, and **gases** are all around us. Look around you. What solids, liquids, and gases do you see?

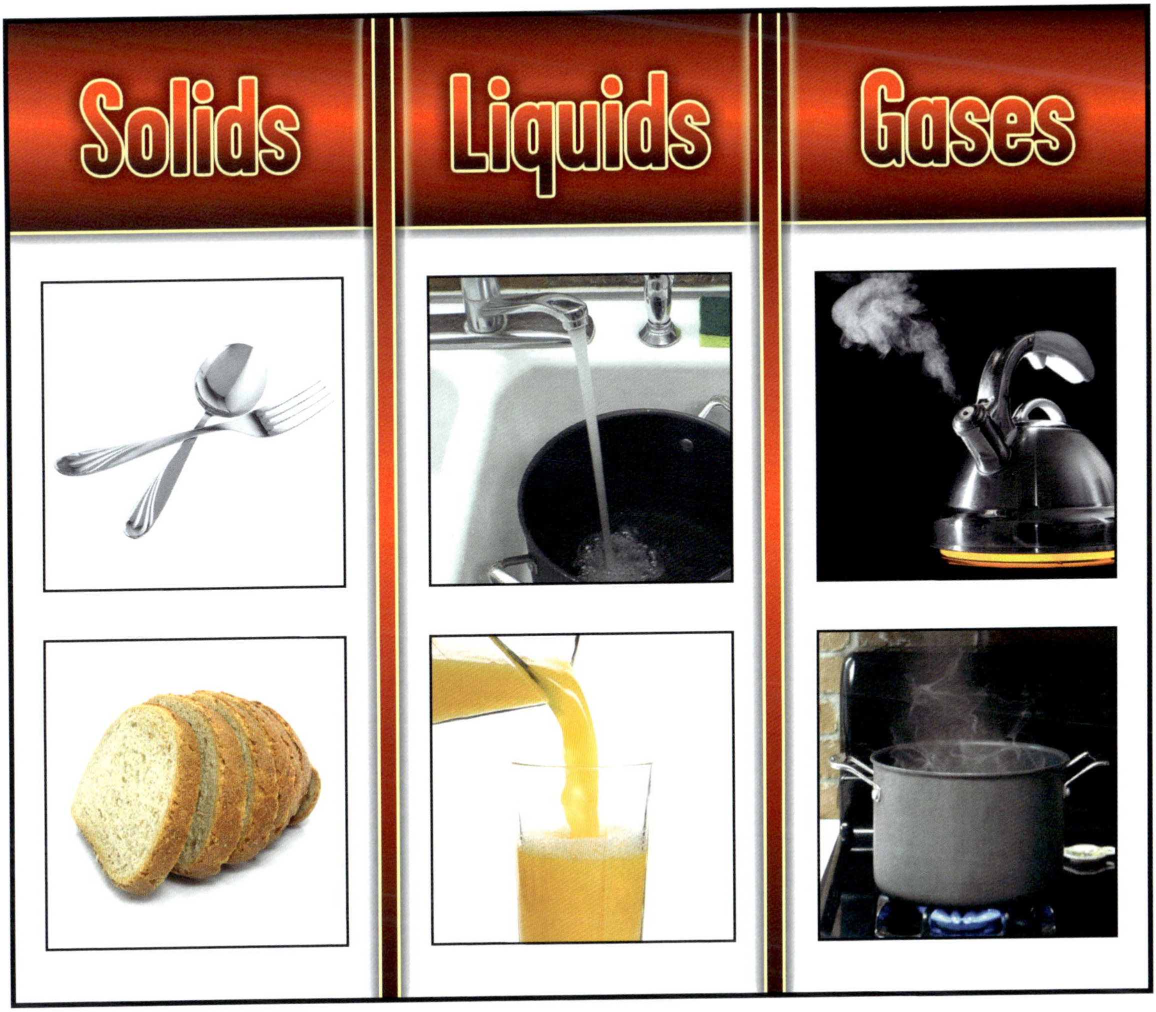

Bread is a solid.

Juice is a liquid.

Steam is a gas.

You can find these in your kitchen!

Water is a liquid.

A liquid has no shape of its own.

It takes the shape of the pot it is in.

Hot water is used to cook some foods.

To heat the water, we put the pot on the stove.

Water gives off steam when it is very hot.

Steam is a gas and has no shape.

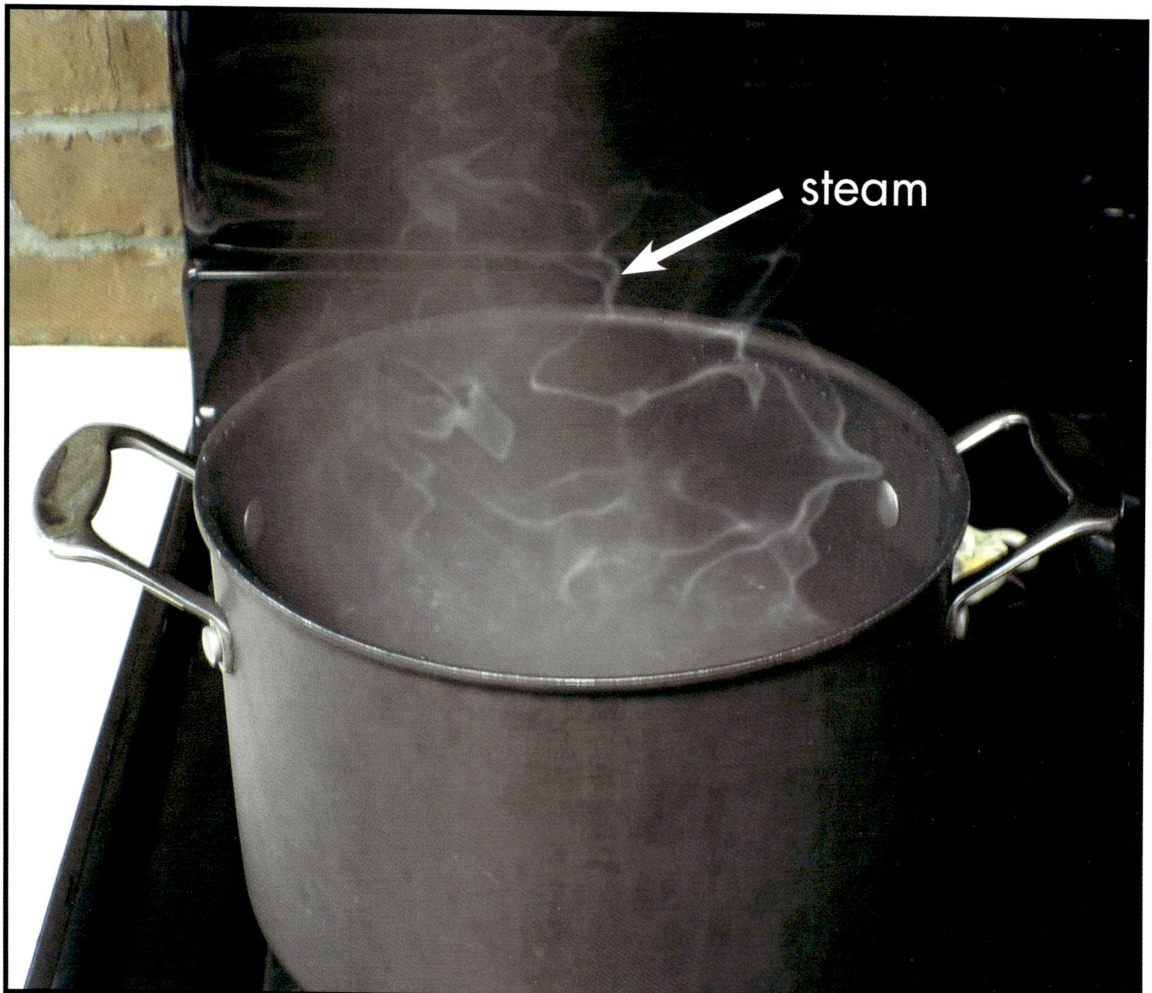

Now the water is ready.

It is time to cook!

Noodles are a solid.

A solid has shape.

You can hold a solid.

Noodles are cooked in hot water.
We put the noodles in the pot.

Soon the noodles are cooked.
Noodles get soft when they are cooked,
but they are still a solid.

Now we know solids, liquids, and gases.

Dinner is ready.

Let's eat!

Glossary

gas Something that has no shape and cannot be held.

liquid Something that flows.

solid Something that has size and shape and can be held.

steam A gas rising from very hot water.